MAN FROM THE SKY

Satchel in one hand, fake pistol in the other, he stepped toward the door. The handle, painted red, stuck upright on the door. Red letters warned: DO NOT TOUCH HANDLE WHILE IN FLIGHT.

For a moment he stood before the door, then shifted his gun to the hand that held the bag. Reaching out with his free hand, he gripped the handle and twisted it.

For a moment it stuck and would not move. Shifting his feet, he gave another yank, throwing all his weight into the twist. As the door moved slightly out, he could feel the sudden change of pressure in the cabin.

He kicked the door, and out it burst, dropping away. Now nothing but the sky was in front of him.

Hurriedly, he dropped the pistol into his jacket pocket, gripped the bag tightly, then dove out of the plane and into the sky.

AVI

MAN FROM THE SKY

A Beech Tree Paperback Book
New York

For Ella

Printed in the United States of America
10 9 8 7 6 5

Library of Congress Cataloging in Publication Data
Avi, 1937–
     Man from the sky/by Avi
         p. cm.
     Summary: In an almost foolproof scheme, a man parachutes
from an airplane with a large amount of money, only to be seen
by a boy who has a reputation for seeing things in the clouds.
     ISBN 0-688-11897-6
     [1. Robbers and outlaws—Fiction.] I. Title.
     [PZ7.953Man 1992]
     [Fic]—dc20
92-1496
CIP
AC

Contents

MAN FROM THE SKY

1

"Can I get it?"

Could I do it?

For the millionth time Ed Goddard asked himself that question.

Could I do it and get away with it?

Leaning forward, he rested his elbows on the top railing of the observation deck at Philadelphia International Airport. Among the many who were watching the jets land and take off, no one noticed him.

Nobody ever notices.

Not very tall, his dark business suit and the tie suggested a man of business. So too did the carefully cut brown hair. The neatly trimmed mustache and beard added dignity, while a round, boyish face with blue eyes and an easy smile gave away no feeling. One would have had to look hard to see the tension in his eyes.

Nobody notices. Nobody bothers to look.

Every Thursday afternoon for the past fourteen weeks, Ed Goddard, former parachutist in the United States Army, had kept his eyes on one spot upon the airport Tarmac. Even as he looked, he again asked himself the question.

Can I get away with it?

He decided to make up his mind that day.

After checking his watch, he looked once more at the Keystone Airlines location. Keystone planes were all Winthrop, two-engine turbo-props. They could hold ten passengers. If the Boeing 747's were the whales of the sky, the Winthrop 220's were the minnows, darting between cities like Philadelphia and places like Elmira, New York, with short runways and few people waiting in the small terminal.

As Ed Goddard watched, six men and a woman stepped from one of the long passenger buildings. For a second they paused, unsure where to go. A mechanic waved them toward the little plane. Seeing only then how small a plane they were about to board, they stopped. Unsureness was written on their faces. Then somebody made a joke, the tension broke, and they moved forward.

Carrying their luggage, they went up an aluminum ladder that hung from the plane. At the top of the steps the co-pilot—no stewardess on an airline the size of Keystone—took boarding passes and welcomed them aboard Flight 74. Stooping, they entered into the small cabin.

Goddard shifted his gaze to the right. He knew what to expect next. A green truck moved heavily toward the Keystone area.

4:05. Three minutes late. Not bad.

Twenty feet from the plane the truck halted. The driver got out, locked his door behind him, then walked carefully to the rear. His hand was on the trigger of his partially withdrawn pistol. At the back door he glanced about suspiciously.

He never looks up here.

The rear door of the truck unlocked, and two men jumped out. One carried a rifle, the other a black leather bag. The bag contained almost a million dollars. All in cash. All in small bills. It was the payroll for the Elmira Box Company, Elmira, New York.

Ed Goddard knew all about the payroll. He knew how much there was, and how it was sent. After leaving the Army he had worked as a security officer at the plant.

Quickly, the man carrying the black bag moved to the plane. Halfway up the ladder, he was met by the co-pilot. The co-pilot took the bag, signed a receipt, laughed at a joke. The guard looked on through the door, the co-pilot locked the bag in a compartment in the rear of the plane.

Just an ordinary lock!

As soon as the guard stepped off the boarding ladder, it was pulled back into the body of the plane. A slight shaking of the door's metal skin told Goddard that it was being closed and secured from inside the plane.

Inside the plane!

Fifty feet in front of the Winthrop, a Keystone mechanic appeared, his ears covered by sound mufflers. He lifted one hand. One engine turned, spun, raced, throttled back. The second motor did the same.

The mechanic flicked both hands back and forth. Slowly, the Winthrop rolled forward onto the runway.

Only then did the guards relax, move back into their van, and drive off, satisfied that all was secure. In Elmira other guards would be waiting to collect the bag.

But in the air, millions of dollars were left unguarded.

At the end of the runway the Winthrop's motors spun faster and faster. Then, getting clearance, the plane leaped down the Tarmac and lifted into the air. Goddard watched until the plane was no more than a speck against the sky.

The only way to get the million was to take it in midair. The only way to get *away* with it was to jump from the plane in midflight.

Once again Goddard asked himself the question.

Can I get it and get away?

For the first time he allowed himself an answer.

Yes, I can. Yes, I will.

The Winthrop 220 was lost in the sky. Goddard smiled. It would not be long before he, too, would be lost in the sky.

Yes, in the sky.

2

"All I'll ever need."

The sky was full.

Jamie Peters, aged eleven, stood out in the middle of the field. Grass, high as his knees, tickled him. But neither the hot air nor the grass bothered him. Head tilted back so that his hair dropped over his shoulders, he was intent upon the sky, staring into it.

And a bright blue sky it was, too, clotted with great clouds. With no trouble at all, Jamie could see marvelous things in the clouds: castles, dragons, knights, powerful horses charging across brilliant blue fields. He saw beautiful ladies, powerful men. When an airplane arched across the sky, he saw a spear being thrown. And Jamie could see it all just by watching the sky.

Better than any books.

"Jamie!"

Out over the long meadow his name floated.

"Jam—ie!"

Jamie tried to ignore the call.

"Jamie!" came the call again, more insistent. Reluctantly, he turned about. "Coming," he shouted. Pausing only to tie his shoelaces, he started to run, his mind still on the people he had seen in the sky.

It was August, hot August, and as he did every year, Jamie had come down from Rochester to spend the month with his grandparents, the Thorntons. His own parents would join him for the last couple of weeks of summer.

Grandpa and Grandma Thornton lived in Pennsylvania, ten miles south of the New York border. Elmira, twenty-five miles to the northeast, was the closest big town.

The land was anything but flat. It rolled up and down like ocean waves, making endless valleys, endless crests. Rocks stuck out everywhere: rock walls, rock patches, just plain rocks. "Boulder gardens," Grandpa Thornton called them. Down the road there was a farm called Iron Acres. The closest town was Job's Corner, which, insisted Grandpa, was meant to tell you how hard things were.

As Jamie came down from the hill he saw his grandmother standing on the porch watching him.

Mrs. Thornton was in her sixties, and to Jamie she was as soft, as easy, as anyone in the world. She was like his mother, but his mother was much more in a rush about things. Grandma Thornton could always take time for him, or the afternoon nap she loved so much.

Jamie, still happy with his visions on the hill, ran up and gave her a hug.

"Now what have I done?" she asked, kissing him on the top of the head.

"Just feeling good," he told her.

"What you been doing?" she asked, as she led him back into the house.

"Sky watching. You know what I saw?"

"Nobody does but you."

"King Arthur and his knights. Sir Lancelot threw a silver spear—fifty miles—and killed the Black Knight!"

"Jamie, you didn't!"

"Did. Really saw it."

She laughed. "You see more things in the sky than most people see on earth."

"I do," he insisted.

"Course you do," she agreed. "How about a snack?" In the kitchen were a glass of milk and a plate with three doughnuts. At home there would only have been one. He took the chair, swallowed half the milk in a gulp, then began on the doughnuts.

"You don't believe me, do you?" he asked, mouth full.

"I do. But you have special eyes. No one can see the way you do."

Jamie, not wishing to talk about it, changed the subject. "What did you call me for?"

"Grandpa had to go over to Mr. Lurie's to help fix a pump. He called to say he forgot a special wrench and could you bring it to him.

You can bike over. He'll drive you back."

"The Luries'?" said Jamie, a note of complaint in his voice.

"Perfectly nice neighbors, Jamie. Do your grandfather a favor."

"Okay," Jamie agreed.

Mrs. Thornton looked about the kitchen. "I wrote out what he wanted, and now I can't find my reading glasses." She slipped a piece of paper across the table toward Jamie. "What did I write?"

Feeling a sudden tightness, Jamie reluctantly picked up the paper on which his grandmother had printed some words. As he studied the letters, he felt himself grow tense. His head began to ache. Trying to remember what the letters were, he stared at the shapes. Dimly recalled, they were unfamiliar. He looked hard at the first:

T

Reaching out with a hand, he pointed above the letter, drew it in the air, or tried to. But it was as if the letter wouldn't stay still.

Line down. Line across.

His own hand became unsteady.

Line down! Line across!

"Oh, Jamie," cried Mrs. Thornton, suddenly remembering. "I am sorry. Give it back."

Feeling shame, keeping his eyes down, Jamie shoved the paper across the table. Taking it, Mrs. Thornton held it at arm's length so she could read. "Two-inch spanner," she read out loud. "Do you know what that is? I don't."

Silently, Jamie nodded.

Yes, she does.

Leaving the last doughnut, he went to the basement, got the tool, shoved it into his back pocket, and went out.

Mrs. Thornton followed him to his bike.

"Jamie," she called softly. "I am sorry. I do sometimes forget, don't I?"

Jamie shrugged.

"Well, maybe you can't read letters," she said cheerfully, "but nobody can read things in the sky like you can. I'm glad you're here with us," she added.

"So am I," he said. "I don't really see those things in the sky, you know," he said, stopping to look up at her. "But I do all the same, sort of."

"It's your way of reading," she replied.

"All I'll ever need to read is up in the sky," he told her.

"Grandpa is waiting," she said with a smile. "Tie your laces and scoot."

3

"I'll do it today."

The apartment on the fourth floor of one of the countless row homes in Philadelphia was small and narrow. It had three rooms: bathroom, small kitchen, and one large room. There in the very middle, Goddard had set up a work table.

That morning he stood over it, jacket and tie thrown off to one side, sleeves rolled up. He stared down at the table on which he had spread an enormous map of the Pennsylvania–New York border area. It was such a large map that the cities, though not in fact very big, appeared as yellow spots on the greater mass of green countryside. Corning, Williamsport, Binghamton, Elmira: names that Goddard had gotten to know from constant study.

On top of the map, over the marks of roads, rivers, town streets, and county borders, ran one red line. It marked the route of the Keystone Airlines Flight 74 from Philadelphia to Elmira.

With his eyes Goddard traced its path. Most of the trip was over empty farmland where few lived. People there would not be very likely to stare up at the sky. By parachuting in the proper place, he could go unseen. *Vanish.* Nobody would even know he had touched earth. And he'd be richer by a million dollars cash.

Turning, he looked at the large stuffed chair in the corner. It held a neatly bound package: his parachute.

Goddard turned back to his map again, trying to learn the names of the towns he hoped to land near. Canoe Landing. Painted Post. Horse Heads. Jersey Shore. Job's Corner. Chumung. Their odd names almost made them easier to learn. He had to learn them so he would know where he was, and then how to get where he needed to go.

After staring at the map for a time, he closed his eyes, saying the names of towns and roads from memory.

The phone rang.

"Yes?" he answered, keeping his voice to a whisper.

"Is this Mr. Robert Lemuel?"

"Yes it is," said Ed Goddard.

"This is Eastway Travel. I have your flight confirmed to Elmira for the twelfth of August."

"The four-fifteen?"

"That's right. Philadelphia International."

"Thank you. Can I send you a money order for it?"

"Sure thing."

"I'll do it right away."

"Have a nice day."

Goddard hung up the phone and drew a notebook from his jacket pocket. Thumbing through the crowded pages, he came to one headed "Ticket Names."

The name *Robert Lemuel* appeared third from the top of ten names. Even as he crossed off that name, the phone rang again.

"Yes?"

"Am I speaking to Mr. David Traxel?"

"That's correct," said Goddard.

"I have Flight 74 confirmed to Elmira for the twelfth of August."

"Keystone Airlines?"

"That's it. Supposed to go at four-fifteen. Be there no later than four."

"Sure. Can I send you a money order for the ticket?"

"Send it right on. This is Lynn, at North Philadelphia Travel Center."

"I'll do it today."

"Bye."

Within three hours, all the seats on Flight 74 to Elmira for August 12 had been reserved, all by Ed Goddard—yet no one by that name had bought a ticket.

For the rest of that day and the next, Goddard studied the map, memorizing it. As he

saw it, there was only one point of risk.
Though he would be jumping into an area
where few people lived, the one danger was
that he would be seen. He doubted he would.
It was, however, the one small risk.

4

"Dreamer."

On his bike, Jamie shot out of the driveway and headed for the Luries'. But it wasn't a bike he was on anymore: it was a motorcycle. Twisting the throttle grips, he made it roar louder.

The hill before the Luries' place was one he couldn't make. Jumping off his bike, he walked to the top. But once there, he re-mounted. Now, however, it was no longer a motorcycle but Pegasus, the flying horse. Without fail it zoomed down to the Luries'.

Mr. Lurie was a dairy farmer with some fifty head of cows on what was mostly rocky pasture. The Luries had kids, too—kids whom Jamie didn't like much. Todd, the Luries' son, was a teen-ager. Gillian was a girl about Jamie's age, while Alice was the family baby.

Parking his bike near his grandfather's pick-up truck, Jamie called, "Grandpa!"

Mr. Thornton stuck his head out of the barn across the way. "Jamie? Got the wrench? Good boy!"

Inside the barn, Mr. Lurie, hands, face, and hair streaked with oil, was on his knees beside the large pump.

For a few moments Jamie stood by, watching, but soon he lost interest. "I'm going outside," he announced. When he came out, Mrs. Lurie was on the porch.

"That you, Jamie?"

"Hi."

"You're bigger than ever. Almost didn't recognize you. How're your folks?"

"Okay."

"Go on out the back, honey, why don't you. Todd's working on his car. Gillian's around somewhere with Alice."

Jamie went round the back, where he

found Todd bending over his 1968 Ford. He had bought it from a junk dealer, and had been trying to get it to go for the past two years. As Jamie appeared, he looked up from his work.

"Hi, Jamie. How you been?"

"Okay. Get it to work yet?"

"Just a few more things to do. Don't worry, I'll get it going."

"What happens if you don't?"

"I just will. What you been doing?"

Jamie shrugged.

"Up for a while?"

"Whole month."

"Hey, you still staring up at the sky?"

Jamie, feeling his face go hot and wishing he had never come, mumbled, "What do you mean?"

"You're big on staring up into the sky, aren't you? I asked your grandmother about it. She said some folks read books, you read the sky. That true?"

"Maybe," said Jamie, concentrating on his shoelace.

"That what they do at that special school you go to, sky read?"

Turning, Jamie started to walk away.

"Hey, Jamie," Todd called after him. "Can't you take a joke?"

Trying not to hear Todd's laugh, Jamie went back to the barn. "Grandpa, I'm going to bike home."

"Won't be long now. I'll drive you."

"I'd rather bike."

"Okay. See you at home then."

Hurriedly, Jamie went back to his bike, only to find that Gillian had come out to the porch. Her little sister, Alice, sat on her lap.

Gillian was a bit taller than Jamie, but her long ponytail made her seem even bigger. Her round, reddish face with its serious look never appeared to smile or to offer much of a welcome. Worse, Jamie could feel by the way she watched him that she found him curious. It was more than enough to make him shy away.

As it was, he only nodded to her, straddled his bike, then pushed back on the kickstand.

"Don't let Todd bug you," Gillian called out in a half whisper.

"He doesn't," Jamie said sullenly.

"Ask him what his grades are."

"He doesn't bother me," insisted Jamie, wanting to leave more than ever.

"Probably a lot worse than your grades," she suggested.

"Yeah," he murmured.

Always telling me how smart I am, then just because I can't read they send me to a school for nonreaders where they aren't even allowed to give grades.

"See you," he called, pressing onto the pedals.

Mrs. Thornton was sitting on the porch chair, reading, when he got home.

"Didn't you want to wait for Grandpa?" she asked.

"Didn't feel like it," he said, parking his bike.

"Where you going now?"

"Just up the hill."

"Reading the sky?" she asked gently.

"Maybe," he returned without stopping. In fact, that was exactly what he was going to do, that and keep away from people who bothered him, like the Luries.

Mrs. Thornton watched him go. As she resumed her reading, she felt her eyes grow heavy.

Dreamer.

Effortlessly, she allowed herself to slip off into her usual afternoon nap.

Dreamer. He's a dreamer.

5

"Everything is ready."

With the greatest of care, Goddard folded his parachute. He did it once, he did it twice, he did it ten times.

No second chances.

It had to be perfect. Each time he folded it, something didn't seem right. Just what, he wasn't sure. But he had learned to respect those feelings, and once more he did the job.

Only when he was completely satisfied did he pack it away, laying it softly on the chair like the precious object it was.

I'll use it tomorrow.

For a few more hours he studied the map, not to learn anything—he was certain he knew it all by heart—but to test his memory. He would flip a coin in the air, letting it fall anywhere along the route the airplane would take.

Who knows which way the wind will blow me?

Taking a quick look to see where the coin fell, he moved to the end of the room. On a piece of paper he wrote out a complete road route to the nearest big town. In doing so, he noted every road he would use, every road he would pass. Then he checked to see if he was right.

No matter where the coin fell, his memory proved correct.

Practice done, he turned on his radio, the radio with the special weather frequency, and listened to the National Weather Service bulletins.

Regardless of the weather, he would go, but he wanted to leave as little as possible to chance. He knew that in his target area summer thunderstorms came and went with great suddenness. But the weather report was good. Fair, hot weather. Only a chance of storms.

During the past week he had removed from

the apartment everything that could possibly be traced to him. Now it stood all but empty. He crossed that task off one of his lists.

At six o'clock in the evening he went down to the basement and knocked on the janitor's door.

"Ah, Mr. Alowski," said the janitor to Ed Goddard. "What can I do for you?"

"I'm going to be away for a while, on vacation," Goddard said. "Just wanted to give you my rent in advance." He handed the janitor a cash-filled envelope.

"Traveling?" asked the janitor as he took the money.

"Visiting my family."

"Now don't worry about a thing, Mr. Alowski," said the janitor. "Hey, do you want me to hold your mail? It's a good thing. People see you don't collect your mail, they know you're away, and presto, a burglar."

"I hadn't thought of that," said Goddard.

"Thanks for the rent," said the janitor. "Hope you have a good time. Going by airplane?"

"Not me," replied Goddard. "I hate to fly."

"Right you are. You might fall down. Have a good trip, Mr. Alowski!"

Upstairs Goddard crossed another item off his list.

In the bathroom he shaved his mustache and beard completely off. It made him look very different. Removing his shirt, he washed his hair and used bleach. In moments he turned blond.

That night he took out the fake pistol, made of wood. Holding it in his hand, he marveled at how real it looked. It even had the right weight. With a few twists of his hands he pulled it apart until six small pieces lay in his hand. It would be impossible to detect as he passed through the electronic barrier at the airport.

He looked at his watch. In less than twenty-four hours he would go.

Everything is ready.

6

"What is he seeing?"

Gillian was standing in the middle of her favorite blackberry patch when she saw Jamie. He had not seen her. But then she was dressed to protect herself from the thorny bushes: dark overalls, long-sleeved shirt, and a kerchief around her hair. To keep her hands free for picking, she had hung a tin bucket by a string around her neck, a bucket already a quarter full. Her fingers were stained deep purple.

When she saw Jamie he was running up toward the top of the next hill. By the way he was going, Gillian could tell that he hadn't the slightest idea that anybody was watching.

At the top of the hill he stood still. Then

slowly, he lifted his arms and tilted his head back.

Gillian had heard about it, but she had never seen him do that before. He reminded her of an ancient statue she had once seen in a school art-history book.

How long can he stay that way?

Watching, she wondered what he was really like. Her brother said he was "weird, standing there, staring at nothing, like some sort of retard." But she had heard Mrs. Thornton tell her mother how smart Jamie was.

As she watched, Jamie began to move, turning slowly in one spot until she could see his face. His arms were still out wide, his eyes stared up, and he was smiling. It looked as if he were flying.

Gillian wanted a closer look. Leaving her bucket on a branch, she moved carefully out from the bush, hoping he wouldn't see her.

As she tried to figure out a way to get close, she noticed an old stone wall that was broken down in only a few places. Here and there trees had grown alongside. By crawling along its length she was sure she could get just below the spot where Jamie was standing.

Running swiftly, she leaped across the one open space, easily reaching the wall. Down on hands and knees she went, then peeked over the stone.

Jamie was still standing there, still turning, eyes upon the clouds.

Gillian crawled behind the wall as fast as she dared until she was only twenty feet from where he stood. Boldly, she sat up on her knees, then leaned on the wall, resting her chin on her arms the better to study him.

What is he seeing?

Without thinking, she stood up, almost daring him to see her. Still he stood as he was, eyes looking elsewhere.

She stepped on the wall, wishing she could do whatever it was he was doing. Then, as she stood there, the wall gave way, collapsing. With a scream, she dropped, sliding on her bottom to the ground until she came to rest, her back against the stone, her feet stretched out in front of her.

Jamie, just as startled, turned to look.

Neither said anything.

Gillian, feeling foolish, slowly picked herself up, untangling her hair from the kerchief, which had almost fallen off.

"Hey!" he called down to her. "You been spying on me?"

"I was picking berries."

"Yeah? Where?"

"Back over there."

Jamie watched her, a frown on his face. "This is my grandpa's farm, you know."

"I always berry here," Gillian answered. "They let me."

He squinted at her. "How long were you watching me?"

"I wasn't watching you," she lied. "I was picking berries. See?" She held up her stained hands.

He thought about what she had said for a moment, then swung about and began to march off. "See ya," he called.

But Gillian was still curious. "Jamie," she called out.

He stopped. "What?"

"What were you doing?" she blurted out.

He shrugged. "Nothing," he said and started off again.

Hurt that he would not talk to her, Gillian ran up to the top of the hill. "I *was* watching," she yelled after him.

He stopped to look back at her. "So what?"

"You don't have to be so stuck up," she answered. "Just because you're from the city and so smart!"

"I hate the city," he informed her.

"I was only asking you what you were doing," she tried. "I never saw anyone do that. Could you teach me?"

"I'm the only one in the whole world who can do it," he announced. And with that, he marched off.

Angry and insulted, Gillian went back down the hill, over the wall, and to her berry patch. Once there she got her bucket and began picking as fast as she could, wanting only to get home soon.

Even so, she made up her mind about one thing: she would come back the next day and learn what he was doing. She was not going to let him—the snob—put her off.

7

"Have a good flight."

At 3:30, Ed Goddard, carrying nothing but his one suitcase, approached the desk of Keystone Airlines at Philadelphia International Airport.

"May I help you?" the desk clerk asked.

"I'm flying the four-fifteen to Elmira."

"Ticket please."

Goddard handed the long ticket to the woman behind the desk as he looked over the lobby area.

No one.

The woman opened the ticket, looked at the name, looked at Goddard: "Mr. Bell?"

"That's right."

"Very good, Mr. Bell," she said, stamping the ticket and handing it back to Goddard along with his boarding pass. "You're all set. We'll announce your flight at about four o'clock. Please have a seat."

Goddard, suitcase on knee, took a place overlooking the Tarmac. The Winthrop 220 was taking fuel from a pump truck.

He waited quietly, trying to be calm, telling himself that he was not nervous.

It'll go perfectly. Everything that I could do I've done. Completely. Carefully.

It was the things not in his control that worried him. Then he reminded himself: if they were things out of his control, there was no point in *his* being worried. There simply was no more he could do.

"May I have your attention, please," came the voice over the speaker. "All passengers holding tickets for Flight Seventy-four, Keystone to Elmira, please go to Gate Six A for boarding."

Goddard went to the gate. The woman who had taken his ticket was there. He presented her with the boarding pass.

"I'm afraid you're the only one," she said with a forced smile. "All the others are no-shows. All of them."

"We'll fly anyway, won't we?" asked Goddard, startled by the suggestion in the woman's words.

"Rain or shine—like the post office," she said more brightly. "No smoking, please, until the Captain gives permission on board," she said, giving him back his pass.

"Thank you," said Goddard. He went down the steps and out onto the Tarmac.

"Over here, buddy," called a mechanic.

Goddard walked toward the Winthrop, pausing only at the foot of the ladder. Looking up, he saw the co-pilot waiting for him.

At the top of the steps Goddard gave up his pass.

"Anyone else?" asked the co-pilot.

"I don't know," said Goddard.

"Take your suitcase?"

"Thanks, no. I'll put it under my seat."

"Sure thing."

Goddard, bending his head under the low ceiling, took a window seat behind the wing. He looked at his watch—4:02.

Turning, he watched outside. Into view came the armored van. The guards did the usual things. Without looking, Goddard knew that one of them was bringing up the money bag.

"That my paycheck?" joked the co-pilot.

"That's the baby," returned the guard. "Don't drop it."

Turning slightly, Goddard saw the money bag placed in the rear compartment. Closing the lid, the co-pilot locked it.

A whining sound, the sound of the steps being pulled in. Then a slam. Locked.

The co-pilot walked by. "You're it," he said to Goddard as he passed. "The whole kit and kaboodle to yourself."

Saying nothing, Goddard watched the co-pilot go into the cockpit, ducking through the small door, shutting and locking it behind him.

Again Goddard looked out the window.

"Ladies and gentlemen," began the hurried voice of the co-pilot over the sound system. "Welcome to Keystone Flight Number Seventy-four, to Elmira, New York. We shall shortly be taking off and should reach Elmira in one hour and thirty-two minutes. Except for the possibility of some thunderclouds we have clear flying all the way. Please take the time to look at the emergency instructions placed directly in front of your seat. Also, please attend to the no-smoking sign and have your seat belt securely fastened. Thank you for flying Keystone, and have a good flight."

Both engines spun.

At the head of the runway the plane waited. Closing his eyes, Goddard pushed himself back into his seat. The turbines roared, quieted momentarily, then the plane began to move faster and faster.

The nose tilted up, and they lifted into the sky.

8

"No one."

Jamie sat staring at the television. But he wasn't really watching. He was thinking about Gillian. He kept wishing she hadn't come to watch him the way she had.

It's my business. None of hers.

He wasn't about to share it with anybody. Nobody believed what he saw anyhow.

People don't understand, not even Grandma. It's not real things that I see.

What he saw were real pictures. Ideas. Exciting ideas.

Better than television. Better than being told stories. Better than reading—my ideas.

He looked up at Spiderman, thinking he could not care less what was on. Getting up, he turned the set off and yawned.

Feeling bored and restless, he walked through the house looking for Mrs. Thornton. She usually had ideas about what to do.

He found her asleep in the living room. She had been reading. The book was on the floor.

Quietly, Jamie went out of the house and onto the porch. He didn't know where his grandfather was. Taking a quick glance at the sky, he saw it was clouding up. Figuring his grandmother would guess where he was, he decided to just take a walk and go look. He was supposed to tell her where he went, to leave a note or something.

Leaving notes is not my way. I'll be back within the hour. Plenty of time before dinner.

At the edge of the yard he stopped, trying to make up his mind which way to go. He wanted to go to his regular place, the one he had gone to yesterday. But Gillian's watching had sort of spoiled it for him.

It's my hill. I'm not going to let her mess it up for me.

Reminding himself that he could watch for her, and that if she was there he could always go somewhere else, he took the path to his hill.

From the pasture he crossed over the back creek. Then he headed for the big rock, a place high enough so he could tell if anybody was watching.

He reached it easily enough, climbed up, and looked about in all directions.

No one.

• • •

Gillian, laying down in the tall grass at the far end of the old orchard, saw Jamie the minute he climbed the rock. Not wanting him to even think she might be out there waiting, she kept low.

As it was, she could tell by the way he moved that he was looking for something. It wasn't hard to guess what—or who—he was looking for either. In spite of herself, she giggled.

At first she hadn't been able to make up her

mind whether to come or not. She supposed it wasn't any of her business. She had even felt a little ashamed about doing it. For that reason she hadn't told anyone where she was going or what she was about to do.

But ever since she'd seen Jamie sky watching she hadn't been able to stop thinking about him. She didn't believe he was dumb or a mental case the way her brother said. When she'd asked her mother about him the night before, all she'd learned was that Mrs. Thornton had spoken of some kind of problem. She didn't know what it was.

As far as Gillian could see, Jamie didn't have any problem. It was just that he knew how to do something she didn't and wouldn't share it with her. She was going to find out what it was.

So she lay there, watching quietly.

• • •

Jamie, on the rock, felt sure that no one was about. He decided he would go to his favorite hill after all. Climbing down, he headed that way.

• • •

Gillian saw him, and certain he was going to the same place she'd seen him at the day before, she bent down low, then ran back toward the old stone wall she had used before.

This time don't make a fool of yourself.

• • •

Jamie plodded slowly up the hill. A breeze ruffled his hair, making the August heat feel lighter. Clouds were piling up quickly to the north, and he wondered if there would be a storm. He loved storms. They provided the most exciting clouds to watch, dark against the light. You could see anything in them.

At the hilltop he stopped, double checking to be sure no one was about. He looked hard at the stone wall, the place where he had discovered Gillian before.

No one.

Setting his feet a little apart, he tilted his head back and with eyes wide open stared into the sky. He waited, just waited, to see what would appear.

9

"I'm ready."

Having reached an altitude of fifteen thousand feet, the Winthrop 220 droned on. Goddard tried to sense where he was by looking below, but he couldn't. It didn't matter.

I'm ready.

Making himself take a deep breath, he drew the black, wooden parts of the pistol from his pocket and snapped them together. He didn't have the slightest desire to use it, but if he had to bluff his way, he would.

A glance toward the front of the plane told him that the pilots were in the cockpit behind their closed door. Happily, he wouldn't even need to bluff.

From under his seat he pulled out his suitcase and removed the parachute. Working quickly but carefully, he stepped into the harness. The straps were drawn tightly, first through his legs, then around his shoulders.

Still, he made himself check the security points three times before he allowed himself to be satisfied.

At the back of the plane he drew out the key ring with its set of locksmith keys. In minutes he found the right key and swung the compartment door open.

The money bag lay inside.

Goddard smiled.

Reaching in, he pulled the bag out. Its weight surprised him.

Lighter than I thought. Better yet.

Carefully, he closed the luggage door, locked it, then broke the key off inside the lock with a quick twist of his hands.

Let them have trouble opening it.

It would give him that much more time.

Satchel in one hand, fake pistol in the other, he stepped toward the door. The handle, painted red, stuck upright on the door.

Red letters warned: DO NOT TOUCH HANDLE WHILE IN FLIGHT.

For a moment he stood before the door, then shifted his gun to the hand that held the bag. Reaching out with his free hand, he gripped the handle and twisted it.

For a moment it stuck and would not move. Shifting his feet, he gave another yank, throwing all his weight into the twist. As the door moved slightly out, he could feel the sudden change of pressure in the cabin.

He kicked the door, and out it burst, dropping away. Now nothing but the sky was in front of him.

Hurriedly, he dropped the pistol into his jacket pocket, gripped the bag tightly, then dove out of the plane and into the sky.

10

"Where has he gone?"

Carefully, Gillian peeked over the stone wall, her eyes intent only on Jamie.

Don't look where he's looking. Don't look at the sky. It's only a fake. Keep your eyes just on him.

• • •

For Jamie, the clouds in the sky were fantastic: boiling, rolling, reaching as high as he had ever seen them, as if they were holding up the sky itself. A sky castle.

To the south, the clouds were the white beings of the planet Mercury, bleached by the sun. From the north came the moving, growing stormclouds—the dark beasts of Jupiter. In their very center he saw splinters of lightning.

Jupiter's fire snakes.

He turned to the south. An airplane, sharp-pointed and silver, cut across the sky.

It was a silver spear from Mercury that . . . .

• • •

Goddard, dropping, felt his heart pounding, each beat marking off the seconds of his free fall. Even as he held the bag, his arms were spread wide, his legs out behind.

Reaching the end of the required count, he yanked at the release cord. A sudden whipping sound told him that the parachute had pulled out freely. A second later it blew completely out, puffed up, until, with a jerk, he was dangling in the air. Hanging from the parachute, he floated down with ease.

• • •

Jamie blinked.

Something seemed to drop from the plane. He watched, puzzled, trying to decide what it was.

At first Jamie thought he had seen smoke. But the smoke took form and shape—a parachute!

A man was coming from the sky.

Jamie spun about, searching all over for the vanishing airplane. Then he swung back to stare at the parachute, which was still dropping. A person hung below.

As it fell, Jamie saw clearly that the person was holding out an arm and from the hand hung a bag or a bundle.

Feeling nothing but excitement, Jamie began to dash toward the spot where he thought the man might land.

• • •

Gillian, her eyes fixed on Jamie, was caught off guard by his sudden movement—not at all the way he had acted before. It was as if he were having a fit, or had seen someone.

She turned around to see if someone else had come, but seeing no one she turned back to where Jamie was standing. But he had gone.

He saw me!

Instantly, she lay down flat against the ground, angry that she had bungled things again. She waited before daring to look up. But when she did, Jamie was still gone. Puzzled, she stood up.

Where had he gone?

• • •

Drawing the money bag closer to his chest, Goddard feeling the fingers of his right hand grow numb switched the bag to his left hand. Only then did he bend over to see where he was headed.

The countryside stretched out like the map he had studied for so long. But now the huge area took him by surprise. He could not tell where he was.

It didn't matter.

He was sure that once on the ground he could easily get his location by finding the first road or town. So he looked to see how the area was populated, happily, noticing that there were only a few farmhouses.

All working perfectly. Just a few more minutes.

Feeling a sudden tug of wind, he twisted his head. Only then did he see the rolling stormclouds bearing in on him.

A piece of bad luck, but nothing more than that. The storm might carry him some distance, and perhaps, if the winds were really strong, it would pull him about on the ground. At the same time, the bad weather made it even more unlikely that anyone would be out to see him drop.

Down he came.

Directly below, the area seemed deserted. It looked like nothing more than an empty, hilly spot.

A cow pasture.

The ground seemed to rush up toward him faster and faster. His left hand gripped the bag loosely, letting it swing.

Safe in seconds.

11

"Find them both!"

Jamie, wanting to be close enough to greet the man from the sky, ran down the other side of the hill. He was trying to figure out where the parachutist would come down, but he was still too far away. And the man was dropping quickly, slipping further away.

"Hey!" Jamie shouted, running as fast as he could and lifting his hand as he went. "Hey!"

Shocked by the sound of a voice, Goddard jerked his head about. Even as he did, the bag, held by his weaker left hand, began to slip.

Twisting suddenly, he tried to grab it with his free hand, only to get caught up in the lines of the parachute.

The satchel began to fall.

Goddard lunged for it, but it was gone, falling like a rock.

• • •

Jamie saw something drop—and he wondered what it was. A thunderclap made him look over his shoulder: the storm was all but overhead. Back he turned to the falling man. He was still dropping, dipping behind the far side of a hill, out of Jamie's sight.

Panting, his side hurting, Jamie tore up the side of the hill, not wanting to lose sight of the man.

• • •

It all happened so quickly: at the moment Goddard caught sight of the kid (he saw instantly that it was a kid), he also tried to see where the bag had fallen. But the storm winds were blowing him down and away too fast, even as the earth seemed to be leaping up to take him. He had to force himself to watch where he was going, trying to steer clear of trees and rocks.

Seeing he was only a few feet away from a landing, he shook his legs, loosening his muscles. Still he struck the ground hard, landing mostly on one leg.

He fell. The parachute, caught by the wind, began to drag. With one quick motion he pulled the release catch. The lines ripped away.

The parachute. Get it before it gives me away.

He staggered to his feet and dove for the lines. Clutching at them, he began to pull the ropes, until with a last hugging motion he gathered them all in, mashing the parachute into a ball.

• • •

Gillian, determined to find where Jamie had gone, walked carefully to the top of the hill and the spot where she had last seen him.

Where's he gone? He saw me for certain. He's hiding from me.

She looked back north and saw the great stormcloud sparked with lightning. A sheet of rain, announced by thunder, was moving closer. Still she waited on the hilltop, seeking some hint of Jamie's whereabouts.

The wind, blowing harder, brought the

first raindrops. Not wanting to get wet, she searched for a place to take cover. Some thick berries at the bottom of the hill looked promising.

Down she dashed. She reached the bushes and dove beneath them. The rain began to pelt down hard.

• • •

Holding the entire parachute with its dangling lines, Goddard stumbled toward some trees. Only then did he realize that the rain had begun. It fell as though dumped from a barrel, chopping at leaves, pounding the ground.

But his thoughts were elsewhere. Somewhere the bag with a million dollars was laying. And a kid had seen him.

Find them. Find them both.

12

"I saw someone."

Jamie stood in the rain for a moment, then ran down the hillside looking for shelter. When he saw a wide pine tree he went for it.

By the time he reached the pine he was soaking wet. Still, the spreading branches were thick enough to keep the rain away. Panting, he sat down on the dry, brown needles.

Then he tried to figure out what he had seen.

It was a man, that much he knew. A man who had parachuted to earth. He remembered, too, that when he had called out, the man had dropped something, a sack, a suitcase, something. Whatever it was had fallen straight down while the man, caught by the storm, blew further on.

Who was he? What did he drop?

Jamie looked out from beneath the tree. The rain was still coming down, but he could see it was slowing, proving to be no more than a thundershower.

He stood up.

Maybe the man was hurt. Maybe he was bailing out of a plane that was about to crash.

But he hadn't seen the plane fall: it had flown on.

If the man was hurt he wouldn't be able to get help for himself. I'll have to get it for him.

Again he looked out at the rain. It was still coming down, but no longer very hard. The thunder had moved on.

Figuring that he couldn't get any wetter than he already was, Jamie moved out from the tree's protection and started to run back toward home. His feet squished against the soaked earth.

Up one hill he ran, down the other side.

And he was dashing across the old orchard when he heard his name called:

"Jamie!"

He turned in the direction of the call. It was Gillian. She was looking up at him on her hands and knees from under a bush.

The moment he realized it was Gillian he started to run toward her, shouting, "Did you see him? Did you? Did you see him?"

"See who?" said Gillian, puzzled.

"The man. The man from the sky. Didn't you see him?"

Gillian sat back on her legs, trying to understand if he was telling the truth or not.

"The man!" he shouted, pointing in the direction he had seen the parachutist drop. "By parachute."

After a moment Gillian said, "You really are crazy, you know. You really are." She pushed herself up.

Jamie, not expecting Gillian's response, stood before her, shocked.

"You stand up there on that hill," she said

to him, "and you just invent things. That's all it is, Mr. Stuckup. A fake."

"He might be hurt," said Jamie, softly.

"He might be King Tut, too," Gillian replied.

"Gillian," he said, "I saw someone. I really did."

"Why don't you tell your grandparents? They can help you look for him." She pushed the hair out from her kerchief and went past him. "See you later. Say hello to your sky man from Gillian."

Unable to talk, Jamie watched as Gillian moved across the field in the direction of her home. But when she reached the top of the hill she turned and stood staring at him.

Right away Jamie decided what she was doing.

Look at her. She's waiting to see if I'm going to do anything. She's challenging me.

He stared back, his anger giving way to frustration.

She was right here and she doesn't believe me. I suppose no one else will either.

There was no choice: he had to find the man himself. He might be badly in need of help.

Angry again, he turned his back on Gillian and began to run toward the place where he thought the man had landed.

13

"Maybe he did see something."

After watching him go, Gillian continued home. Uneasy, she couldn't get Jamie out of her thoughts.

Why is he acting that way to me? He really is crazy.

It was as if he were testing her. Yet, in other ways, he seemed ordinary enough. It made no sense to her. She continued on, but her steps grew shorter.

Maybe he did see something. He certainly was excited, different than he was.

She stopped and looked back. The rain had become no more than a mist. In the little valleys at the bottom of hills, the earth seemed to steam. But Jamie was out of sight.

With a shake of her head she started walking again.

I wasn't watching the sky. I kept my eyes on him. What if he did see something?

Unhappy with herself as much as with him, she again stopped.

I'm a dope.

With that thought she turned about and moved back, once more going to the top of the hill from which she had just come. From up there she could just see Jamie disappearing over a bluff.

He's going somewhere.

Knowing that if she went around the same hill she would come out along the line in which he was going, but wouldn't have to show herself, she sighed. She looked at the sky. It was perfectly clear and dry. "I'm stupid," she said out loud. "Stupid as he is!"

With a reminder to herself that she had not told anybody where she was going and that she had to get home soon, she started off after him.

14

"Which way to go?"

Ed Goddard pushed the dead leaves over what remained of his parachute, hiding it.

One less piece of evidence to be found.

He stood back from the pile. As he did, he felt a pain in his knee. He knew that he must have twisted it when he hit the ground.

Nothing to do about it.

He looked out from behind the trees. Only low hills met his eyes, hills broken by small groves of trees and rock piles. In the many valleys, bushes fed on runoff water.

Swearing out loud, Goddard made himself think of what to do.

Find the kid or find the money?

He checked the time. In four hours it would be dark. That didn't give him much freedom. By now they would have discovered what had happened on the plane. He knew the search for him had certainly begun. If a public announcement was made it would bring out lots of lookers, people hunting for the money or him. Worse: how long would it take before the kid who had seen him told? It would bring the searchers on even faster.

A million bucks out there.

That decided it for Goddard. He would look for the money, get it, and get out.

Which way to go?

He tried to remember the order of events. Which way he had been blown? How long before he landed had he dropped the bag?

Slowly, he moved out into the open, heading for the spot where he had come down. When he reached it, he tried to get his position. Had he been blown north or south?

On a distant hill not too far away he noticed a large pine, which rose higher than the other trees. He remembered that he had seen it while coming down.

The other directions he studied gave no

better idea of where he was, so he headed for the tree. Walking as fast as his sore knee allowed, he kept up a sweeping search for the money bag. It could be anywhere.

A hopeless feeling made him stop. He felt like crying. It had all worked so well except that some kid had been standing out in the field.

One kid!

Shaking his head, he forced down his feelings, knowing they would make his search more difficult. The bag—with its million dollars—*was* somewhere. All he had to do was find it, find it first.

Pushing on, Goddard continued until out of the corner of his eye he saw a black lump upon the ground. His heart bounding, he stopped.

It was up the hill to his right, against a gray boulder. Excitedly, he started to run toward it. His knee reacted with pain and he made himself walk. Halfway there he saw the object for what it was—a rock.

Tired, he continued on anyway, kicking the

stone in disgust when he reached it.

He looked down at himself: shirt, jacket, tie—wet, covered with mud, and he in the middle of a field looking for his million.

In spite of himself he laughed.

For a moment he sat down, resting. When he got up he continued in his earlier direction. He had taken only five steps down the hill when he saw Jamie coming around some trees.

Instantly, he flung himself upon the ground. And only with great care did he lift his head and look. Jamie, below, couldn't see him.

Is that the kid?

Everything had happened so quickly that he could not be sure.

Again he peered up at the boy. Jamie had come to a stop. He seemed to be making up his mind which way to go.

He's looking for something. Is he looking for me?

Goddard pressed himself flat against the ground. As he lay there, he was struck by the thought that if it *was* this boy who had seen him, then clearly he had not gone to any house. Not enough time had passed. And that meant that—other than this boy—no one yet knew about him.

But is this the boy who saw me?

Again Goddard lifted his head. Jamie had started to move in a direction that was taking him further away.

Let him go.

In moments he was gone.

The fact that the boy had come and left was taken as a good sign by Goddard.

I'll get out of it yet.

Standing, Goddard turned back in the direction he had first been moving, toward the pine tree, continuing his search for the bag as he went. Even so, every now and then he glanced over his shoulder just in case the boy came back.

15

"Better to just leave it."

Gillian walked along easily, carelessly.

The whole thing is stupid. I'm a ninny, too.

Swinging her hands as she walked, she pulled at a tall spear of grass, yanked it off the stem, then chewed it without thinking as she pushed on.

Stopping, she looked about. Jamie was nowhere in sight. Worse, she had no idea where he might have gone, none.

Maybe he's only tricking me. I deserve it for being so nosy.

That thought was enough to make her decide to go only as far as the next hilltop. Then she would go home. Reaching it, she stood tall, slowly turning a full circle to look at the land about her.

No one.

With a slight toss of her hair away from her eyes and swearing that she didn't care, she started to come down. As she did she saw something odd.

At first she wasn't sure what it was: black, sort of round, stuck in between two gray rocks. She only discovered it because of the way in which she came toward the rock. Any other way and she would have missed it completely.

Twenty feet from the rocks she stood trying to guess what the object was. But she couldn't.

Curious, she moved toward it. By the time she had covered half the distance, she realized what it was: a leather bag.

Stopping, she just looked at it. It was so oddly placed that she couldn't help but wonder how it got there. Perhaps it was Jamie's secret hiding place.

Better to just leave it.

Her curiosity, however, was too great. She went up to it and looked closer. It wasn't any cheap plastic bag, but a bag made of real leather with a metal strap around it, all held together by a lock. But the lock had opened.

Without thinking, she climbed up on the rocks, reached down, grabbed the bag's handle, and pulled. It would not come loose.

Stretching down with her other hand, she leaned on the rock, then yanked with her full weight. The bag began to move. Again she pulled. Each effort made it slip a little more. With a final pull, it popped out so quickly she fell back, while the bag dropped to the ground on one side. The top sprang open. Bundles of money spilled out onto the wet ground.

Hardly believing what she was seeing, Gillian just stared at the money. Then she bent down and picked up one of the bundles.

Money. Real money. A lot of money.

She stood up, half expecting that someone would be watching what she was doing.

No one. No one at all.

Moving with an immediate sense of something important happening, Gillian pushed the bills back into the bag. With both arms she picked it up, held it in a comfortable way, then began to walk home. But then she stopped.

Maybe I shouldn't take it. It must belong to someone.

Again she looked about.

No one. It can't be Jamie's.

Deciding that she had better get home as quickly as possible, she held the bag even tighter and began to walk quickly.

16

"Wait!"

Ed Goddard stood in the middle of the field. As far as he could see there was nothing but hills. Rising and falling, they made it impossible for him to see any great distance. Whatever break in the hills he could see was cut by either trees or rocks.

Hard country.

He patted his knee, still painful.

I can't let it end this way.

A look at his watch made him realize how little time he had. By now they certainly had started hunting for him. He looked up, almost expecting to see low-flying state police helicopters sweeping along the route the Keystone plane had taken. They would be searching for some sign, any sign.

They won't find the parachute. And I can easily get away so they'll never see or find me. But the money. A million dollars. Laying out there. Near. Somewhere.

He paced off another hill.

As he walked, his body twisted about, trying to check the widest possible area. When he reached the top of a hill he turned about in a full circle.

It was then that he saw Gillian.

She was moving quickly in one of the valleys. She was carrying something in her arms, just what he couldn't tell at first. As he watched her, his first thought was that she was the boy he had already seen. Only when Gillian turned slightly did he realize it was not the same person.

A girl.

Once again he tried to remember the kid who had hailed him as he dropped, more than willing to believe that this was the one. As he studied her he suddenly realized that she was carrying the bag.

Instantly he jumped to his feet and shouted: "Hey! You there!"

Below, Gillian stopped and searched out the voice, squinting up to where Goddard was standing.

"You!" Goddard called. "Wait!" And he began to lope down the hill, paying no heed to his knee.

17

"Do something!"

Gillian had been completely surprised by the voice. For a second she had thought it was Jamie calling. She saw soon enough that it wasn't the boy at all, but a man she had never seen before.

Meeting anyone there would have been startling enough. But the man she was looking at was dressed so oddly, in a suit, a torn, filthy, disheveled suit. His hands, equally dirty, were held out as if to prevent her from moving. Worse, the hard stare of his tension-filled eyes made her feel immediate fear and caused her to back up a step. Even so, she responded to the adult command and stayed where she was.

Goddard rushed down to within a few feet

of where she stood, then stopped. For a moment he simply looked at her.

Gillian saw at once that what he was most interested in was the bag she was holding in front of her.

"Better let me have that," he said, reaching out a hand. "It's mine!"

The violence in his voice made Gillian back up against a rock.

"Didn't you hear me!" he shouted, and with a lunge he ripped the bag from her grasp.

"Don't you move," he told her, though Gillian was still standing right by him, too frightened to budge, a sense of awful sickness rising up inside her.

"Where'd you find it?" he demanded.

"Over there," she whispered out of a tight throat. "In the rocks."

"Did you see it fall?"

Not understanding what he was asking, she only looked at him, her eyes wide.

"I said, 'Did you see it fall?' " he repeated, his voice rising.

She shook her head, no.

"But you saw me land, didn't you?" he shouted, his own emotion making him tremble with anger.

"I don't understand you," Gillian insisted, feeling bewildered. His face, for all his anger, told her nothing of who he was, what he was doing there, or what he wanted of her. The blond, short hair, the smooth face, the blue eyes, seemed the worse to her for not saying anything.

"You saw me land when I parachuted. From the sky, you idiot! I saw you!"

Only then did Gillian realize who the man was: he was the man Jamie had tried to tell her about, the man from the sky.

Jamie was telling the truth.

"I didn't see you," she managed to say.

"The hell you didn't. I know you did," he cried. "Don't lie!"

Gillian, feeling the tears in her eyes, only bit her lip.

Goddard abruptly shifted his gaze and looked about. "What is this place?" he demanded. "What's the nearest town?"

"Job's Corner," she whispered.

"Job's Corner," he repeated, eyes closing for a moment as he studied the map in his memory.

"Mansfield is five miles from here," he shouted out. "Springfield is eight."

She nodded, yes.

"How far's the road?"

"Not far."

"But there's a bus in Mansfield, isn't there? Am I right? *Answer me!*"

"Yes."

"Okay," he said. "Now listen: you're going to show me how to get to Mansfield. Not by road. I don't want roads now. They'll be watching the roads by now. Can you get me there without roads?"

"I don't know," she said honestly.

Losing all patience, Goddard took his wooden pistol from his pocket.

"Listen here, I've got to get to Mansfield and it has to be in a hurry. You're the one who's going to show me how to do it. You understand me?"

She nodded, yes.

"Okay," he said, calming down. "Just do that and it will all be fine. I'm not going to hurt you. But don't fool around. Don't run away. I've got to get this whole thing together."

Gillian, trembling, watched as Goddard put the bag down, looked inside, closed it, then began to fiddle with the broken lock.

Her legs unsteady, she sat down on the ground, her back against the rock. She stared at the man, not really believing what was happening, what he was doing, or where she was.

Because he had a gun, she felt there was nothing she could do to get away from him. Carefully, she looked about in the slight hope that Jamie might appear.

No one.

If she could at least tell Jamie where they were going, leave some clue, some message, it might help. And if he found it he could go get someone.

Do something!

She stole a look at Goddard. He was tying the arms of his jacket into a knot around the bag.

Drawing up her knees, Gillian bent her head down, as if resting. With her feet to hide what she was doing, she quickly began to write with a finger in the damp dirt. First she drew an arrow. Then she began to spell out the word *Mansfield*.

→ MANS

"Hey!" he called.

She jumped.

"Let's go!"

Fearful that he might see what she had done, she got up instantly, hiding the marks with her body.

Goddard waved the gun at her. "Come on. You're going to lead the way. Come on!"

Not daring to look anyplace but where he pointed her, Gillian did as told.

18

"What does it say?"

Discouraged at finding nothing, Jamie sat down to rest.

Maybe I am crazy. Maybe I didn't see anything.

He picked up a pebble from the ground and flung it away. At the spot where it landed a grasshopper jumped straight up into the air, rattled its wings frantically, only to land a few feet away.

He looked up at the sky.

No clouds at all. Nothing to look at.

Discouraged, he got to his feet and decided he might as well go home.

He walked slowly, almost sorry that he had to go. His grandmother would listen to his story, would smile and be interested. But she wouldn't believe him either. He was beginning not to believe himself.

If there was a man with a parachute, where did he go? Where did he disappear? If he had been hurt, he would have cried out. Perhaps he died.

Making his way slowly to the top of the next hill, he stopped to look about. Across the field, in the valley below, he saw Gillian and Goddard.

They were near a large rock. Gillian was sitting with her back against it. The man was busy with something on the ground.

Jamie watched as the man gathered up a bundle, then stood. He seemed to say something to Gillian, who got up quickly.

Jamie, wanting to call, felt his mouth open, but before he could get out a sound he was stunned to see the man point a gun at Gillian.

Shocked into dumb silence, he stood there until, unable to support himself, he dropped to his knees. Even so, if Goddard or Gillian had turned, they would have seen him. As it was, they were too intent on where they were moving.

They started to move away, and Jamie turned his head as if to seek another witness to what he was seeing. Finding no one, he turned back. It was enough to set his mind churning frantically.

Is that the man I saw drop from the sky?

He thought it was.

What's he doing with Gillian?

His heart beating painfully enough to make his chest ache, he watched them for as long as he could. Only when they moved behind some bushes and disappeared from view did he move. Then he hurled himself down the hill to the place where they had been, reaching it in minutes.

Trying to catch his breath, he looked in the direction they had taken. He tried to make some sense of why they had gone that way, but his head was too full of questions. The questions chased one another like swirling leaves.

Where are they going? What's going to happen? Should I follow? What can I do? Nothing!

Upset because he could not think what to do, he let himself slide down the face of the rock to the ground. The only thing he could think of doing was to run back home, tell his grandparents what he had seen, and just hope they believed him.

But where can I tell them they were going? If there's nothing to tell them, they won't believe me.

Absentmindedly he bent over to tie his shoelace; it was then that he saw Gillian's marks. Immediately he swung around to take a better look.

$$\longrightarrow \text{MANS}$$

Letters. Writing.

And, as always, when he saw writing and tried to make sense of it, his head began to hurt.

It must have been Gillian who wrote it. She was sitting here. She must have been leaving a message. What did it say?

→ MANS

It has to mean something. I have to know what it means.

He stared at the marks. He knew he had seen them before, many times. Now, before his eyes, they seemed to twist their shapes like live snakes that wouldn't stay still long enough to be captured. He made every effort to keep them still, but they refused to help.

Putting out his hand, he held it over the first letter, tracing its shape in the air. The second. The third. The last.

The second one. Pointy. With a cross line. That's the most familiar one. Start with that. Pointy with a line.

On the ground where Gillian had scratched

her letters, Jamie retraced the lines with his own hand.

"*A!*" he said out loud. "*A. Ah! A!*"

His heart racing with the excitement of discovery, he sensed that he had been correct. Knowing it made the letter stay still. It was as if he had tamed it.

I know the second letter.

But the first and third letters still escaped him, seeming to be much the same—yet different.

M N

He traced the first letter, *M*, below the one Gillian had written.

He glanced up at the sky.

Make them clouds. Make them clouds!

Closing his eyes, Jamie tried to repeat the shapes in his mind, then looked up at the sky and marked the first one anew against the sky.

The feeling of it began to drift through his mind.

Mmmmmmmmm

"*M!*" he shouted.

Instantly, he tried to put the first two letters together. "*M—A—Mmmmm—Ahhh.*"

It doesn't work.

Worried, he returned to the third letter. It was so much like the first that it made his head throb. What other letter was like *M*? "*W!*" he said out loud.

The letter shook.

It wasn't right.

Again he stared up at the sky.

If it were in the clouds I could see it.

"*N,*" he whispered. "*N! Nnnnnnn.*"

Hitting the ground with his fist he tried to put the three sounds together: "*Mmmmm—*

Ahhh—Nnnn." He repeated the sounds over and over again, closing his eyes tightly, listening to his own noise.

"Man. Man. Man!" he shouted.

The last letter.

S

His head was not hurting nearly as much as it had. It seemed as if he could see this last one better, more clearly. The wiggly one, the snakelike one . . . . "*Ssss* . . . ."

"*S!*"

"*Mans!*"

But it was like leaping off a cliff: after all that effort there was nothing. The word meant nothing at all.

It's a word I don't know.

Again he studied what Gillian had written, the arrow, the letters, reading it over and over again: "Mans, mans, mans, mans . . . ." The arrow pointing toward the letters.

Going toward the letters. Going toward . . . .
. . . . Mans . . . . Two going pictures . . . . Going

Mans . . . one meaning . . . . Going mans . . .

Like a picture against the sky he saw it: *Going to Mansfield!*

Leaping to his feet he shouted up to the sky: "Going to Mansfield!" And Jamie began to race toward home.

"Going to Mansfield!" he shouted again.

19

"I'm not fooling."

Through the front door of the Thorntons' house Jamie burst. Grandpa was sitting, watching the TV news.

"Where's Grandma?" Jamie called.

"In the kitchen."

"Grandma!" Jamie called as he ran into the next room.

"There you are!" exclaimed Mrs. Thornton, looking up from the newspaper she had been reading. "I was just beginning to think I should get worried." A single dinner setting for Jamie was on the table.

"Grandma, listen," cried Jamie. "I was watching the sky when I saw this man parachute from an airplane. I looked for him but couldn't find him. But then he caught hold of Gillian, Gillian Lurie. He's got a gun. He's making her go to Mansfield."

Grandma Thornton smiled as she began to set Jamie's dinner out. "Well, it's not dragons and knights this time. Did you get caught in the storm?"

"I'm not fooling, Grandma! It's the truth. It really is!"

"I'm sure you saw it, Jamie. You see more things than a fly with a thousand eyes. Now change your clothes while I set out dinner."

"Call the Luries," insisted Jamie, holding the phone to her. "Ask them if Gillian is there."

"When I am ready, Jamie, I'll call. For goodness sake, do you know what time it is?"

"I'm telling the truth!" shouted Jamie.

"Jamie," said Grandma softly, but stiffly. "I don't like it when people shout. Please."

Grandpa Thornton stood in the doorway. "What's all this shouting about?"

"The boy's upset," said Mrs. Thornton. "He says—it's one of his sky stories—that he saw a man, a man mind you, come from the sky.

Says the man captured Gillian Lurie and has taken her off to Mansfield. With a gun, too."

Mr. Thornton frowned. "What do you mean from the sky, Jamie?"

"A parachute!" exclaimed Jamie. "Out in the field. I really saw him. And he and Gillian are going to Mansfield."

"How do you know it's Mansfield, Jamie?" put in Grandma. "That's a few miles off."

"Gillian left a message. I read it."

"*Read it*, Jamie?" said Grandma, becoming annoyed.

"You don't believe me," cried Jamie. "But I really did read it. Mansfield. An arrow, *M-A-N-S*."

"Just a minute," said Grandpa Thornton. "Jamie, you said a man parachuted from an airplane. Is that it?"

"That's what the boy said. Jamie, I want you to calm yourself."

"Just now," continued Grandpa, "a fellow on the TV news was telling something like that. Seems that on a flight to Elmira, mind you, Elmira, they were carrying a whole bag of money. Seems some guy took it and jumped out between Elmira and Philadelphia."

"You see!" cried Jamie, in victory. "I told you!"

Mrs. Thornton went to the phone and dialed the Luries' house. "Mrs. Lurie? Jane Thornton here. Is your Gillian home? I see. Now, I don't mean to alarm you, but Jamie just ripped in here telling us . . ." And she repeated his story. When she hung up she looked first at Jamie, then at her husband.

"I think we had best call the police," she said.

20

"What about the girl?"

As soon as the call was put through, Grandpa Thornton told Jamie to follow him to his truck. First they headed for the Luries' house, where Mrs. Lurie got in. Then again they tore off.

Cutting through back roads they reached the crossroad of Highway 16 and Route 12 in less than five minutes. A state trooper's car was waiting.

Greeting them with few words, the trooper asked Jamie and Mrs. Lurie to get into his car. Promising to call Mr. Thornton as soon as any information came to hand, they started off.

While Mrs. Lurie sat in the back seat, Jamie,

up front, told the trooper the whole story as he remembered it.

"Was this man carrying anything, son?" the trooper wanted to know.

"A kind of bundle, I think."

"And I understand you believe he had a gun. Is that correct?"

"It looked like it."

From the back seat Jamie heard Mrs. Lurie whisper, "Oh my God." He knew she was trying to hold it back, but she was crying.

"She'll be okay, Mrs. Lurie," the trooper promised her. But even as he spoke, he picked up the hand microphone on the dashboard and began to relay the information Jamie had given him. From time to time Jamie corrected him when he got the facts wrong.

The patrol car, its lights flashing and siren screaming when it had to pass another car, raced to the northern outskirts of Mansfield. There they met up with other police cars. All the officers conferred.

"Could you recognize this man if you saw him again?" Jamie was asked.

"I think so."

"Give us what you can, a description."

Jamie provided the best he could while the policemen took notes.

"What about the girl?"

Mrs. Lurie, her eyes red but no longer tearful, described Gillian. Jamie watched her hand as she constantly mashed a handkerchief.

"Okay," said the trooper in charge. "You'll go in one car with me," he said to Jamie. "Mrs. Lurie, we'd appreciate it if you'd go in another. If they were heading for Mansfield we should be able to spot them."

"They *are* heading for Mansfield," insisted Jamie.

21

"If only Jamie went to get help."

Goddard kept Gillian moving a few paces in front of him. He had instructed her to keep away from all roads and houses, and she had done just as he had asked.

"Where are we?" he asked after they had gone a good while.

Gillian stopped and looked back at Goddard. "We've come about two miles."

"You sure this is the fastest way?"

"Yes, sir."

He shifted the wooden gun to the hand that held the bundle. "All right." But as Gillian started to move again he changed his mind. "Wait a minute."

She stopped.

"We can rest a while. Go on, sit down." Gillian did as she was told, and Goddard sat himself down on a rock, his bundle on his lap. With his free hand he rubbed his knee.

"What's your name?" he asked.

"Gillian."

"Gillian what?"

"Gillian Lurie."

He nodded toward the bundle. "You know what's in this?"

She nodded. "Money."

"You know how I got it?"

"No."

"You wouldn't believe how hard I worked for it. Worked for almost a whole year." He shook his head as if he couldn't believe it himself.

Gillian, her immediate fears beginning to ebb, looked closely at Goddard. She could see he was exhausted just from the way his hands hung down. She had often seen her mother and father look that way after they'd worked until late at night.

But he must be a crook.

"What's your father do?" he suddenly asked her.

"Dairy farmer," she replied.

"He rich?"

"No."

Goddard started to smile. *I'm rich.*

"When I get home I'm going to go on vacation. Sit on the beach in Florida. Do you know how I got here?" he asked.

She shook her head, no.

"Yes, you do," he snapped, his anger returning. "You saw me parachute down. Don't tell me you didn't."

He's thinking about Jamie. He thinks I'm him. It's good that he does. If only Jamie went to get help.

"Don't tell me you didn't," repeated Goddard.

"Yes, I did," said Gillian.

"Damn right, you did!"

Gillian studied his face.

He's proud of what he's done.

Goddard stood up. "Three miles to Mansfield," he announced.

Then he closed his eyes in concentration. "We could go to Springfield," he suddenly said. "If they knew where I landed they'd figure I'd go to Mansfield. They wouldn't even think of Springfield."

Gillian's heart began to beat hard.

If we go to Springfield my message won't mean anything.

"It's further," she quickly said. "And much more rocky."

He looked at her, and for the first time he smiled. "You're right," he said. "And my knee hurts. Let's go to Mansfield."

Gillian got right up.

"Gillian," he said.

Surprised that he used her name, she turned back.

"It's going to be all right."

Once more she began to lead the way.

22

"What if I got it wrong?"

As soon as Jamie settled into the front seat of the trooper's car, they began to move.

"You must have been all shook up when you saw what you were telling us about," said the trooper.

Jamie shrugged. "I guess so."

"You did the right thing."

"Thank you."

"How long did it take you to figure out the message?"

Jamie stared straight ahead down the road. "Not long," he mumbled.

"I just hope you read it right," the trooper said casually.

Jamie shook his head in annoyance.

What if I got it wrong?

"I read it right," he said out loud.

Once in town the car slowed down as it began to cruise through the back ways. Then up and down the main roads it went, constantly returning to the center of town. But once there, the trooper returned the car to the side streets.

It was growing dark.

• • •

Gillian reached the hilltop first. In the dark, the lights of Mansfield lit up the valley below. Goddard joined her and stood by her side.

"Good girl," he said, with a sigh.

For a moment they just looked.

"Can I go home now?" she asked softly.

Goddard shook his head. "The bus station, Gillian. Show me the bus station and that'll be it. Do you know where it is?"

"I think so."

"That's all I need. Come on."

Resigned, Gillian began to lead the way down the hill.

Jamie, be in Mansfield. Be in Mansfield.

Goddard, his weariness growing, called to

her. "Hey, not so fast." And he put a hand on her shoulder.

Don't want her to run away now.

She could feel the gun under his hand.

• • •

For more than an hour Jamie and the trooper continued at the same slow rate they had been moving. Neither had seen anything. Worse, in the dark, the only things they could see were framed within their headlights. Exhausted, Jamie slumped back in his seat, eyes staring ahead.

"Maybe you were wrong," said the trooper softly.

I wasn't wrong.

Despite his effort to keep his eyes open, Jamie could feel them beginning to close. Once he did doze, and he felt his head drop forward. He jerked it back.

The trooper flipped on a blower. A cool breeze blew into Jamie's face, reviving him.

Mansfield. It read Mansfield.

His head felt heavy and he was no longer sure if he was awake or asleep, dreaming. In his dream he saw Gillian again, and by her side, was the man.

He snapped his head up.

"There!" he shouted, pointing down the road. The trooper slammed on his brakes, throwing Jamie forward against his seat belt.

Along the sidewalk, side by side, Goddard and Gillian were coming toward them. He was limping, carrying a bundle with one arm. His other hand, still holding the gun, was on Gillian's shoulder.

The squeal of the trooper's car stopping made Goddard look up and stop, eyes alert. Momentarily his hand lifted from Gillian's shoulder. In that instant, she sprang away.

He made a grab at her, but she had moved too quickly and was running toward the lights.

With a yank, Jamie pulled back the door handle and jumped out. "Gillian!" he shouted. "Here!"

Just as quickly, the trooper sprang out from his side, his gun drawn and aimed at Goddard.

"Don't move!" he cried.

For a moment Goddard stood motionless, surrounded by the light. Filthy, exhausted, he stood clutching the bag. With a flip of his wrist he flung the gun onto the pavement. It landed with a wooden clatter.

The trooper, edging forward, came close enough to pick it up.

Still Goddard remained motionless, peering into the light. Standing, staring at him, shadows against the light, he could see the trooper, Gillian, and a boy.

It's him. The boy!

With a grunt, he pulled open the bag and turned it over. Bills poured out and lay at his feet. He was still gazing at the pyramid of money when the trooper gripped his arm.

Jamie looked at Goddard. *I bet I looked that way when they asked me to read.*

23

"Don't you see them?"

Overhead the clouds were piling up. Jamie, head thrown back, arms extended, began to see what he was looking for and started to call out.

"The good knight is rushing forward, his lance down. The evil knight is holding his ground. Don't you see them?"

Gillian, standing right next to him, mimicking his gestures, was also staring up into the sky of clouds.

"Don't you see them?" Jamie repeated.

"I see something different," she shouted back.

"What?"

"Letters. All twenty-six of them. Look, there's a fantastic *Q*. And a *Z*."

"Where?"

"Right there, crazy. In those clouds."

Jamie, turning to where Gillian was pointing, began to laugh.

I'll see them too!